# THE ADVENTURES of Glibb Redundant

## THE SHORTCUT

Ken Blanton

Copyright © 2024 **BlantonBooks Publishing**

All rights reserved. No part of this publication may be reproduced, distributed, or transmitted in any form or by any means, including photocopying, recording, or other electronic or mechanical methods, without the prior written permission of the publisher, except in the case of brief quotations embodied in critical reviews and certain other noncommercial uses permitted by copyright law. For permission requests, write to the publisher, addressed "Attention: Book Rights and Permission," at the address below.

Published in the United States of America

ISBN 978-1-963379-45-7 (SC)

**BlantonBooks Publishing**
222 West 6th Street
Suite 400, San Pedro, CA, 90731
http://kenblantonbooks.com.

Ordering Information and Rights Permission:

Quantity sales. Special discounts might be available on quantity purchases by corporations, associations, and others. For details, contact the publisher at the address above.

For Book Rights Adaptation and other Rights Permission. Call us at toll-free 1-888-945-8513 or send us an email at okbky69@aol.com

Once upon a time, there was an eight year old named Glibb Redundant. He lived with his mother and father in the country, on the outskirts of town. He had to walk to school in the rain and snow as well as on good weather days.

One particular morning, he prepared to walk to school, as usual, by himself. He stood on the porch and noticed that it has rained the night before. There was mud everywhere! The clay could suck his shoes right off his feet. The teacher would be angry with him if he got mud in the school hallway and classroom floor.

Glibb knew that there would be mud puddles and lots of mud on the side of the main road. He walked down the driveway, dodging the puddles, and turned in the direction toward school using the side of the main road.

Glibb was trying to stay out of the mud on the side of the road but realized it was very muddy today. It seemed to be much more muddy than usual when it rained. He started thinking again of the problems he might encounter, walking the regular way to school, wishing there was another way to go. He then realized that there was a road that he had never been on before, just ahead on his left side. It seemed to be less muddy, and he could see grass growing on it in places. The road seemed to go straight to school instead of winding around as the main road. It might be shorter and less muddy, Glibb was thinking. Glibb had a decision to make now, as he had approached the road that turned off to the left, which seemed to be less muddy and a shorter route to school. It was so muddy this morning that the mud would be on his shoes and take a lot of time to clean before the school bell would ring and he might be late getting to his classroom. Glibb decided to take the shortcut to school.

Glibb recalled what his mother had said just that morning after straightening his shirt and helping him put on his jacket just prior to leaving for school. She said, "Dodge the mud and mud puddles and get to school on time. Stay on the main road, and do not take any shortcuts, son." She then handed Glibb his school books and book strap. He made sure the strap was tight around his books so they would not fall into the mud if he had to jump a puddle. Glibb thought that his mom would never know that he disobeyed her and took the short cut to school anyway.

Glibb inspected his shoes, as they seemed five pounds heavier already. The mud had already caked onto his shoes. He found a stick at the roadside and began scraping off the mud. Now that he was on the shortcut, he realized the roadway had grass growing on it not very far ahead, so, he started dragging his feet to remove the mud from the bottoms of his shoes. He had never used this road to get to school before. He again recalled that his mother had instructed him not to take a shortcut to school but to stay on the main road before he left home this morning.

Glibb was happy to once again have mud from his shoes. It would be a closer route to school than going the main road, he decided. He continued on the shortcut for several minutes and realized a fence was placed across the road not very far ahead. When he got to the fence, he looked both ways to see if there was an easier way to cross. There were bushes, vines, and briars growing up the fence everywhere but directly in front of him, Glibb realized that it was the best place to cross the fence. The vines would surely have thorns, and he wanted nothing to do with them.

Glibb decided to climb the fence. He first tossed his books over so he could use both hands to climb. He saw that his books landed in a mud puddle on the other side. Glibb was almost over the fence when his pant leg got caught. He thought he was going to be late for school, so Glibb jerked up and down to free himself and heard a ripping sound. His pant leg tore, but he was free to finish climbing the fence. Glibb decided the tear was not very large and that his efforts had paid off. He had saved some time and would get to school on time.

He was standing on the ground, on the other side of the fence, and picked up his books from the mud puddle. He used the corner of his jacket to wipe the water from his books. He tightened his strap around his books diligently and turned quickly to continue on to school. He was at the edge of the puddle, and the mud was slick. One leg went north and the other went south as he slipped from his feet, falling into the puddle. Glibb found himself sitting in the cold muddy water of the puddle with his books over his shoulder. He had mud caked on the seat of his pants and the back of his jacket.

Glibb managed to get to his feet again without getting his books in the mud. He decided that his clothes would dry before he arrived at school. Time was wasting, and he had to get to school on time no matter what. Glibb continued down the path on the other side of the fence, as the road was overgrown with bushes and tall weeds except for the narrow path.

There were many beautiful birds singing their songs as Glibb walked by close to them. There were red, blue, yellow, and also multicolored birds along the way. The birds were of all different sizes and sounded so good that Glibb wished he had time to stay and watch and listen, but he had to get to school on time.

Glibb walked down the path for a time and saw a clearing ahead. There was a fence in the distance. Glibb thought that this was no shortcut with the fences he had to climb to get to school on time. He was not saving much time climbing fences and getting snagged on them.

Glibb came to the fence and looked on the other side for a safe place to put his books, to enable him to use both hands for climbing the fence. He looked the fence over to ensure that he would climb it and not again get his pant leg snagged. He was about to throw his books over the fence when he heard pounding thumps getting louder behind him.

A gigantic bull, the size of a house, was charging toward him. He dropped his books and climbed the fence in record time. He climbed so fast that he was on the ground before he realized his books were still on the other side of the fence. While he was climbing the fence, a dog appeared and distracted the bull. The dog began barking and distracted the bull, giving Glibb time to find a stick and pull his books under the fence to grab them.

The dog knew where to crawl under the fence and did so after Glibb had reclaimed his books. Glibb thanked the dog and considered the dog his friend. The dog and Glibb continued on toward school together. The dog acted as if he belonged to Glibb. They walked on quickly to get to school on time, with the dog leading the way. Glibb kept thinking that he could not be late for school. After the fence, again, there was another narrow path. The dog would turn his head back toward Glibb to see if Glibb was still following.

The stream was not supposed to be a part of Glibb's shortcut, but there it was. It was swollen from the rains and overflowed its banks. It was too late to turn back and take the muddy main road to school. He did not want to climb fences or again deal with a bull.

Glibb looked both ways and thought he saw a bridge ahead. He was not completely sure but decided to take a chance on it. Again, the dog led the way up a narrow path, which was not very far from the swollen stream's excess waters. Weeds and bushes with briars and thorns were overhanging the path. The dog was leading the way as if he knew the way over the stream. He had Glibb convinced that he did, and Glibb continued to follow the dog.

The briars and thorns scratched Glibb's hands and ankles, and his legs and arms through his clothes. There were all kinds of Critters scurrying in different directions from the path as the dog and Glibb approached. Glibb noticed a skunk on the path ahead and quickly called the dog to him and stooped down, petting him to distract the dog. This gave the skunk time to go away. He has heard stories about how smelly-a skunk could make you. The skunk had enough time to mosey on.

Glibb stopped petting the dog, and they continued on their search for a way over the swollen stream. Glibb saw several critters along the path. There were rabbits, squirrels, a turtle, and several frogs. He heard several other sounds of critters scurrying under the bushes by the path but did not see what was making each noise. He continued to follow the dog up the narrow path for quite a while. Glibb was sure he had enough time to get to school on time once he spotted the bridge ahead over the swollen stream.

Glibb was concerned when he got close enough to see that the water was flowing over the top of the bridge. The bridge was very old, and the water was several inches deep and swift as it flowed over the deck of the bridge. The bushes were much thicker continuing up the bank path, with briars and thorns, so he knew he had to cross the bridge. While Glibb was pondering what to do, the dog had crossed and was waiting for him on the other side.

The dog was drinking the water while waiting for Glibb to cross. Glibb commenced crossing the bridge and realized how cold the water was as it soaked his shoes and pants to his knees. The bridge seemed to go on forever, but finally, he got to the other side.

The trail ahead was still a narrow path but had no briars and thorns as the previous path. The birds continued to sing their songs, and there was a gentle breeze, and Glibb was shivering from being wet.

Glibb walked faster down the narrow path. After a while, the narrow path opened up into a field. It was mowed short and was a large, open area. The dog barked at Glibb and then ran off to a house sitting back at the edge of the woods. Glibb noticed a road ahead that could be a driveway. He figured that the dog lived at the house and that the driveway would take him to the main road and to school on time.

Glibb decided that the muddy main road would not be so bad to walk down. The dog disappeared at the house, and Glibb arrived at the driveway. Glibb turned away from the house and started down the driveway, hopeful it would lead him to the main road.

Glibb found that the driveway turned to the right and then to the left and back to the right. It seemed to go on and on, but he kept walking. He walked for quite a while on the driveway before he heard a loud truck. The sound went from left to right as it passed. He could hear it, but the trees and thick bushes kept him from seeing what it was or if it was on the main road.

Glibb was very happy to see the main road after such a long driveway. He was not sure that he was going the right direction. He could get to school on time and maybe play kickball if he was there early enough. Then it dawned on him that he had no idea as to which way his school was on the main road. It seemed like a much longer route taking the shortcut.

He decided to flip a quarter to decide which way to go. Heads would mean he would go left, and tails would mean he would go right. He had seen his dad do this to decide a matter. He flipped the coin into the air, and he did not catch it as it landed in the tall grass. He saw where it fell, so he parted the grass. He eventually found the coin with the head side showing. He started walking to the left down the road toward school.

He put his lunch money back in his pocket as he walked. He was busy trying to dodge the mud and puddles as a big truck came by and splashed muddy water all over Glibb. He was glad he was looking the other way when the big truck came by. The mud went everywhere and covered him and his books. His cap and jacket were wet and covered with mud.

Glibb wished he had time to go home and change his clothes, as he was very uncomfortable and his shoes made funny sounds as he walked. His ankles, wrists, and arms were burning and itching from the thorns and briar scratches from the narrow paths, and his pants kept sticking to him. He tried to ignore it all and kept walking, as he needed to get to school on time.

"Boy, what a shortcut," he said. He just listened to the birds singing and saw an occasional car go by as he walked. Glibb was again contemplating going home, changing his clothes, and getting clean again.

Meanwhile, a school bus approached going the other way. The school bus came to a stop beside Glibb, and the doors opened. The driver honked the horn. Glibb looked up to the bus driver, whom he recognized from the office at his school. Glibb was very glad to climb on the bus. The driver immediately realized how muddy and wet Glibb was. He told him to stand by the doors and hold on to the silver bars. The driver did not want to have to clean his bus any more than was necessary. The driver asked Glibb how he got to be such a mess. Before Glibb could answer, the driver asked him where he was going, as he was going the wrong way to get to school.

Glibb said, "I walk to school every day but today I took a shortcut. When I got to the main road, I did not know which way to go, so I flipped a quarter, and the wrong way won. A big truck came by and splashed mud and water all over me. I thought I might get muddy either way, but not this bad," Glibb explained.

The driver pointed toward the school. Children were playing kickball and running around. Other busses were unloading as the driver pulled in the driveway. The children were whispering about Glibb and giggling as they got off the bus.

He saw the teachers walking up the sidewalk of the school's front door and knew school would start soon.  Once the driver had parked the bus and turned it off, he told Glibb to follow him. They went to the front door of the school.

"Wait here and I will be back in a minute," the driver said. After the bus driver was gone what seemed like a long time, Glibb decided he would be late for class if he waited any longer. He had to go to the bathroom and wash his muddy hands. By the time the bus driver returned to where Glibb was to be waiting, Glibb had gone somewhere. He had left Glibb there only a short time. The bus driver had informed the office of the muddy boy and was asked to bring him. The bus driver threw up his hands and started walking to his bus. He thought the office could locate a muddy little boy, but he had no time to hunt for him.

He reasoned that the child was in school somewhere.

Glibb opened the door to the school and was walking down the hallway when the first bell rang. He did not see the driver anywhere, so he continued to the bathroom. He had not gone very far down the hall when the door opened and several children came in at a fast pace. They pushed Glibb into the bulletin board, and the mud went all over it.  Glibb and his teacher had just put most of the things on the bulletin board the day before. Now the mud had covered most of what was there and could not be read through the mud coating.

He knew he had less than five minutes to get to class before being tardy once the next bell rang. He decided to not wash his hands but to go to class. Maybe his teacher, Miss Smith, might not realize how wet and muddy he was.  Some of his classmates noticed him and came to see why he was so messy.

"I took a shortcut to school", he said.

He continued to walk toward class. He looked behind him down the hall and saw a trail of muddy footprints. He decided to continue to class.

A voice called to him from down the hall. It Was Miss Smith, his teacher. The tardy bell rang. She was late for class too, he thought. Miss Smith noticed how muddy and wet Glibb was and saw the mud on the hallway floor. Then she noticed the muddy bulletin board.

"What happened to you, Glibb?" she shrieked,

"I took a shortcut to school, ma'am" Glibb answered.

As she came closer, she noticed the mud still caked to his pants and jacket. She decided to take him to the office. Miss Smith called Glibb's mother to take him home, but she did not answer.

Miss Smith told Glibb, "Sit here in this chair until I get back". The janitor heard her and told Glibb, "Wait. Here is a rag to sit on".

The rag was spread over the chair, and Glibb sat down. The janitor went back to the hallway to clean the mud from the floor. Glibb sat there on the lumpy rag and the caked mud on his pants for what seemed like an eternity to him. He could hear the mop hitting the side of the mop bucket from time to time while waiting for his teacher to try call his mother again. Miss Smith came and tried to call his mother again and finally contacted her. She said she would be there shortly.

Miss Smith told Glibb, "Your mother will be here in a few minutes, so stay there until she picks you up to take you home.

"Yes, ma'am," Glibb said.

Miss Smith talked to the secretary for a short time and turned and left the office. Glibb squirmed and got as comfortable as possible. His mind wandered as he waited for his mother.

He recalled last summer's visit with his aunt and uncle in north Florida. He had tried to catch a chicken and fell several times into a big mud puddle. He never caught the Chicken, because the chickens on the farm were much faster than him.

His aunt and uncle have a very nice farm, with a beautiful white house, two barns, cows, horses and chickens. Glib recalled how important he felt when asked to open the farm gates for his uncle each time he went from field to field on the tractor. Glibb would ride on the tractor with his uncle when feeding the livestock or checking the fencing. He enjoyed helping his uncle on the farm. He would help his uncle count his cows and would have the wrong total because the cows would not stand still.

Glibb's aunt would laugh when Glibb would fall into the mud puddle while chasing the chickens. She would then wash him off with the garden hose before having him to take a bath. He missed them and their farm.

About that time, Glibb's mother arrived and had to snap her fingers to get his attention. He was deep into his thoughts and did not realize his mother had arrived and was now talking to the secretary. She turned back to Glibb and looked him up and down and shook her head in disbelief. Glibb realized he was in trouble. His mother made him get the big rag he was sitting on for protection of her car seat. Then they left school for home.

Glibb was trying not to think about how upset his mother was and wondered if his toes would look like prunes since they had been wet all morning.

By the time they arrived home, the mud was drying and falling onto the car seat and the floor. Glibb did not sit still, and some of the mud was ground into the seat fabric. His mother parked the car in the garage, and they got out. He was instructed to take all his clothes off before he went into the house to bathe in the upstairs bathroom. He finished taking the wet and muddy clothes off and started upstairs. His mother was angry with him, he figured, since she said nothing to him but instructions.

Mom will tell dad I disobeyed her, and boy will I be in trouble, Glibb thought.

Glibb arrived in the upstairs bathroom with his shriveled toes and got into the tub to take a bath. His mother was outside, rinsing out the mud from his clothes.

Today was wash day, and she would have been almost done if Glibb would have still been at school.

Glibb was almost finished bathing when he realized he had not washed his muddy hair. He had forgotten the shampoo, and it seemed just out of reach on the bathroom counter. He realized that his mom and dad would expect him to have put the shampoo close before getting in the tub.

They would tell him not to stretch to get the shampoo from the tub. The bottle was new and the top was opened. It would surely spill if it would tumble onto the floor. Glibb decided that he would stay in the tub, as he was sure he could reach the bottle. He noticed his clean, dry clothes placed on the cabinet, ready for him, and the towel on top of them. He tried to stretch to get the shampoo and got the bottle in his wet hand. It slipped and landed just far enough from the tub. Again, he thought he could retrieve it without getting out of the tub. He almost had it, and then he slipped and fell out of the tub right onto the shampoo bottle. It squirted everywhere. The new bottle was almost empty. It was on the floor, the sink, and the mirror. The wall was not spared either.

A mess can happen very quickly sometimes, he thought. He realized the mess needed to be cleaned up soon, as he was in enough trouble already. He saw a new roll of toilet paper and bunched a lot of it in a ball.

It came apart and did not clean the shampoo well. He grabbed the shampoo bottle and turned to go to the tub, and his feet slipped out from under him.

He fell. He still had the bottles in his hand, and he crawled back to the tub. He started to wash his hair when his mother came in. She took two quick steps toward the bathtub and stepped into the shampoo mess on the floor. Boom! She slipped and crashed to the floor. His mother carefully got up and said, "Wait until your father gets home." Then she walked carefully out of the bathroom.

She went back downstairs to get lunch ready. Glibb could see she was very upset with him for disobeying her and causing a mess in the bathroom. Glibb had rinsed the shampoo from his hair and stretched over to get the towel to dry himself. Glibb's father arrived home, and he smelled lunch cooking. He went to the bathroom to wash his hands. he stepped into the shampoo mess. Boom!

There he sat on the floor. He scratched his head, trying to figure what had happened. Glibb was still in the tub drying off when his father slipped and crashed to the floor. Glibb laughed, which was not appreciated by his father. He looked at Glibb with disbelief.

"How did you accomplish this? Why are you home and not at school?" his father chided.

Glibb responded sheepishly, "I took a shortcut to school this morning. I fell into a mud puddle, got chased by a bull, and got soaked crossing a stream. Then I fell out of the tub trying to get the shampoo, and I fell onto the shampoo bottle."

His father was not listening but trying to stand up as he held onto the sink cabinet. His father shook his head and said, "when I was your age, I had to walk to school much farther than you. I walked to school in all kinds of weather for miles, uphill both ways! I never had to go home in the middle of the day to clean up and change clothes!" his father stated.

Glibb thought he was smart to not mention ripping his pants while climbing the fence.

His father looked back at him once he was safely out of the bathroom. "Get dressed and come downstairs to lunch. After lunch, we will have a talk."

Glibb threw his towel onto the floor and tried to clean up the shampoo. He also used it on the sink and wall, but it did not work too well on the mirror. Atleast he could walk on the floor without falling. He got dressed and went downstairs for lunch.

They were both sitting at the table, waiting for Glibb. His father said grace, and then they ate lunch. Nobody said very much through the meal.

Once lunch was over, Glibb's father said, "Glibb, let us go outside and get a breath of air and you can tell me all about your day so far. You must have had a very interesting morning." His father did not seem angry but curious.

After they were outside, Glibb started telling the story from the beginning. He said that he realized none of it would have happened if he would have done as his mother had asked him that morning. He just wanted to dodge the mud puddles. He again conveyed the shampoo episode to his father, and his father listened. Glibb was sure that his father was aware that he arrived at school on time, although he was sent home with his mother. His father tried not to laugh at first, but it was all funny, except the part where Glibb did not obey his mother.

His father recalled some of the experiences he had encountered at Glibb's age. After Glibb was finished with his story, his father took over the conversation.

"Son, it rains every now and then. This is the only time you got so muddy and wet going to school. It happened because you did not obey your mother. The shampoo accident happened because you did not plan ahead and put it close enough that you could reach it without getting out of the tub. You should think all things through before doing anything. Most of all, you should always mind your mother and me, as we will never tell you anything wrong. You will not get into trouble if you listen and obey us and do as we tell you. I believe you have learned your lesson today, as I see all the scratches on your hands and legs. The wet shoes and mud was punishment as well. I will not punish you further as long as you have learned your lesson. Glibb, go to the garage and get the fishing poles and tackle out so we can go fishing tomorrow at the pond. It has been a while since we have gone fishing, son."

Printed by Libri Plureos GmbH in Hamburg, Germany